kind

bitty ☆ baby
and me

by Kirby Larson
& Sue Cornelison

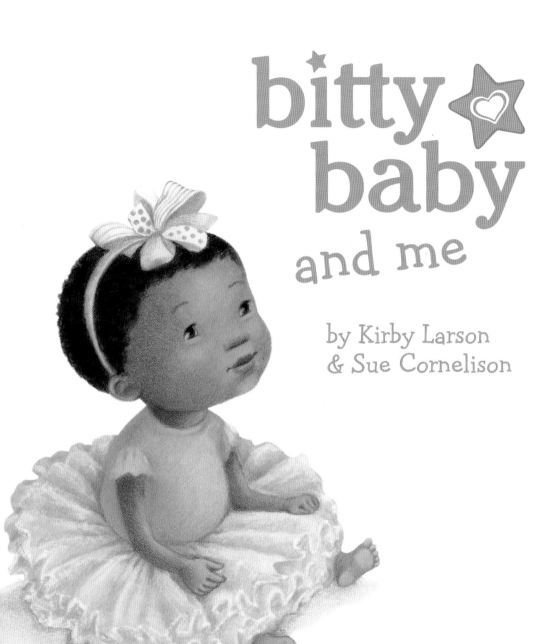

☆ American Girl®

Special thanks to Dr. Laurie Zelinger, consultant,
child psychologist, and registered play therapist.
Dr. Zelinger reviewed and helped shape the "For Parents"
section, which was written by editorial staff.

Published by American Girl Publishing
Copyright © 2013 by American Girl

Questions or comments? Call 1-800-845-0005,
visit **americangirl.com,** or write to Customer Service,
American Girl, 8400 Fairway Place, Middleton, WI 53562-0497.

Printed in China
13 14 15 16 17 18 19 20 LEO 10 9 8 7 6 5 4 3 2 1

All American Girl and Bitty Baby marks are trademarks of American Girl.

Series Editorial Development: Jennifer Hirsch & Elizabeth Ansfield
Art Direction and Design: Gretchen Becker
Production: Tami Kepler, Judith Lary, Paula Moon, Kristi Tabrizi

Cataloging-in-Publication Data available from the Library of Congress

For Esme

K.L.

For my sisters, Lynn and Kathy

S.C.

Bitty Baby and I hopped out
of bed. Mommy and Daddy
were being sleepyheads.

"Who is this?" asked Daddy.

"Bitty Baby," I said. "And
she's ready for breakfast."

"I like pancakes,"
I said to Bitty Baby.
"The smiley-face
kind. Do you?"

She did!

Bitty Baby and I ate every bite of our breakfast. "Bitty Baby says thank you," I said.

"What lovely manners," said Mommy. "Now, do you want to get dressed? Grandma sent matching tutus for you and your new doll."

Bitty Baby and I raced to the bedroom
to try on the new clothes.

We twirled in our tutus. "We look like ballerinas," I said.

"Almost," said Bitty Baby. "Ballerinas wear special shoes."

"And sparkly crowns," I said. "Ta-da!"

"We're dressed," I told Mommy. "Now what shall we do?"

"I bet Fifi would like to say hello,"
said Mommy.

Bitty Baby and I went over to Fifi's bowl.

"You can feed her,"
I said. I showed Bitty Baby
how to take one pinch of fish
flakes. Only one. "Good job,
Bitty Baby," I said.

Fifi blew fish kisses
to Bitty Baby. She
blew baby kisses back.

Keep Out
This means You!

"Do you have any other animals?" asked Bitty Baby.

"No," I said. "But I have a big sister."

We peeked in her bedroom.

"Go away," said my sister. "Can't you read?"

We closed the door.

"Is she a porcupine?" Bitty Baby asked.

"No, she just looks like that in the morning," I said. "Would you like to see my swing set?"

We went outside.

"Do you want the first turn on the swing?" I asked.

"Let's swing together," said Bitty Baby.

We both fit, just right, in the swing. I showed Bitty Baby how to pump. Then Mommy called us in for lunch.

"Bitty Baby likes bananas on her peanut butter sandwich," I told Mommy.

"Dolls don't eat bananas," said my big sister. "Or peanut butter sandwiches."

"Bitty Baby does," I said. Bitty Baby and I ate up every bite.

"Now what shall we do?" I asked.

"I'm going to do a jigsaw puzzle," said my big sister.

Bitty Baby and I looked at each other. "Can we help?"

"You're too little," said my big sister. "Besides, it's time for your nap."

"Do we have to?" I asked.

"At least a rest," said Mommy.

Bitty Baby and I fit together, just right, in my bed. I gave her a kiss and sang a sleepy-bye song.

But it was hard to rest. Bitty Baby was too wiggly.

"Sometimes when I'm wiggly, Mommy tells me a story," I said. "Maybe if I tell a story, you won't be so wiggly."

Bitty Baby clapped her hands. "I love stories!"

We snuggled under the covers.

"I'll tell you about a little girl who lived with a nice mommy and daddy and a prickly porcupine."

The little girl loved her family, even the porcupine, but sometimes they were too busy to play. And most of the time, the porcupine was too prickly to do anything.

One night, the little girl made a wish on the first twinkly star she saw. She wished for a special friend. The next morning, there was Bitty Baby!

"Hi," said
Bitty Baby.

"I made a wish on a
star last night for a
special friend."

"I made that same wish!"
said the little girl.

"Do you like puzzles?" asked Bitty Baby.

"I'm very good at puzzles," said the little girl. "Do you like playing mermaids?"

"Glub-glub," said Bitty Baby.

"Let's play dress-up!" said the little girl and Bitty Baby at exactly the same time.

They put on some mermaid clothes. They invited the porcupine to swim under the sea.

"We're going to see turtles
and sea stars," said Bitty Baby.

"And maybe even a whale!"
said the little girl.

"There's no such thing as
mermaids," said the porcupine.

"Now there are!" said the little girl.
She and Bitty Baby dipped and
darted and swam and splashed.
They dived so deep that
they found a pirate's
treasure chest!

They swam up to
show the porcupine.

"Look what we found!" said Bitty Baby.

"Do you want to do this puzzle with us?" asked the little girl.

"You can't do puzzles," said the porcupine. "They're for big kids."

Bitty Baby and the little girl did puzzles and played until bedtime.

"Look, there's a twinkly star," said the little girl.

"Let's make a wish," said Bitty Baby. "Let's wish that we will always be best friends."

And their wish came true! Bitty Baby and the little girl were best friends. Forever. The end.

Bitty Baby smiled. "You tell good stories," she said.

"Thank you," I said. "And rest time is over! Now what shall we do?"

"I have an idea!" said Bitty Baby. She whispered in my ear.

"That's a great idea," I said.

Bitty Baby and I colored and glued and made a sparkly, twinkly star. Then we made another wish.

We slid our wish under my sister's bedroom door.

And guess what?
That wish came true, too.

For Parents

The Power of Stories

Every child loves a story. Stories let you and your little one share cuddly, intimate time together. By opening a child's eyes to new possibilities, stories are a great way to help her work through anxieties, provide wish fulfillment, and encourage positive behavior.

While there are many wonderful children's books, when you make up a story, you can create characters and situations just for your child. The story can be as realistic or fantastical as you like; just make sure the main character solves her challenges successfully, for a happy ending.

Here are some examples of how a story might address a common issue in a little girl's life.

Anxiety

Is your girl worried about a parent taking a business trip? Make up a story about a mommy or daddy who goes away. Describe the interesting things that happen—both to the traveling parent and to the girl at home—and the joyful reunion at the end. Or, if she's afraid of monsters, tell a story of a monster who tries to growl but burps instead! When you help a child laugh in the face of fear, you defuse its power.

Relationships

Is your daughter shy about making a new friend? Tell a story about two little girls (with the names of your daughter and her friend,

of course) and their marvelous trip to the zoo—or to the moon! Your story will show her how to make—and be—a friend.

Wish Fulfillment

Does your girl long for a pony? Make up a story about a girl and her pony. If you live in the city, here's your chance to describe some of the challenges of keeping a pony in the city. Maybe the pony has to live in the bathroom and eat hay out of the bathtub!

Positive Behavior

Is there something you'd like your little one to get better at, such as brushing her teeth or putting away her toys? Tell a story that teaches the lesson you need—about a little beaver who wouldn't brush his teeth and got a toothache, or messy Marissa moth, who couldn't go out flying because she couldn't find her wings. If your daughter gets impatient with her baby brother, your story could feature a baby boy who wins a gold medal for being the silliest baby in the world—and a sister who wins a gold medal for teaching her little brother so many new things.

Some nights, let *her* tell *you* a story. Make a point of listening without interrupting or inserting your ideas. Her tale will give you insights into her interests, her worries, and how she thinks. Just as the little girl in *Bitty Baby and Me* solves her problem with her prickly sister, your daughter may find her own answers by trying them out first in the safety of her mind, with you by her side.

For more parent tips, visit **americangirl.com/BittyParents**